Should I Share My Ice Cream?

To Diane Camp
for always sharing her enthusiasm

ISBN 978-1-338-34358-8

12 11 10 9 8 7 6 5 4 3 2 1 18 19 20 21 22 23

Printed in the U.S.A. 40

First Scholastic printing, September 2018

This book is set in Century/Monotype; Grilled Cheese/Fontbros; Typography of Coop, Neutraface/House Industries.

Should I Share My Ice Cream?

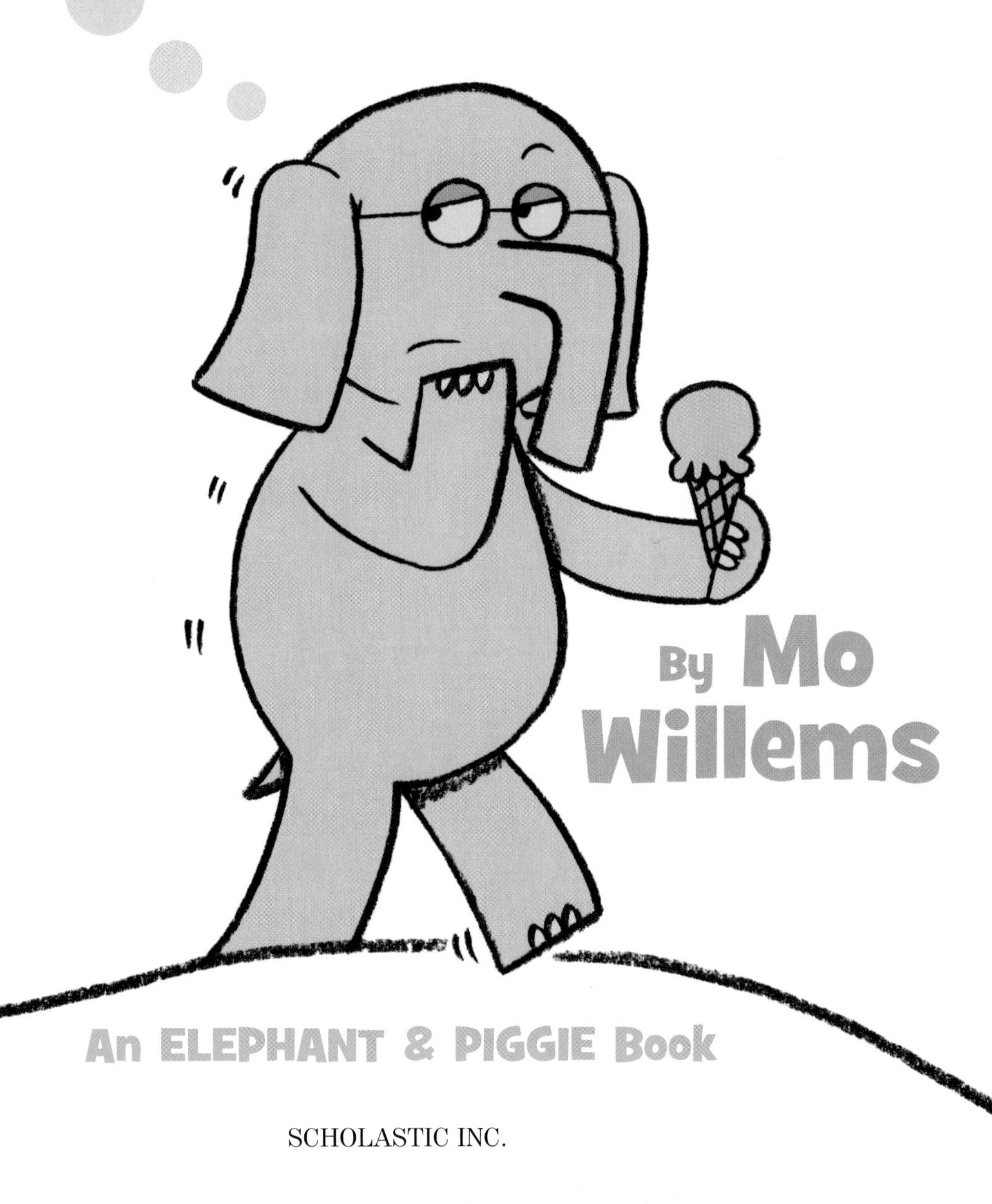

By Mo Willems

An ELEPHANT & PIGGIE Book

SCHOLASTIC INC.

Ice cream!
Get your cold
ice cream
for a hot day!

Oh, boy!
Ice cream!

One ice cream,
please.
Ice Cream!

Here you go!
Ice Cream!

Oh, boy!
Oh, boy!

I *love* ice cream!

Wait!

Piggie loves
ice cream, too.

Piggie is
my best friend.

Should I share
my ice cream
with her?

Should
I share my
awesome,
yummy,
sweet,
super,
great,
tasty,
nice,
cool
ice
cream?

Hmmm...

mmm...

…mmmMMM!

Maybe Piggie
does not like
this flavor!

Sharing a flavor
Piggie does not like
would be *wrong*.

I will eat the ice cream!

Wait.

Piggie will like
this flavor.

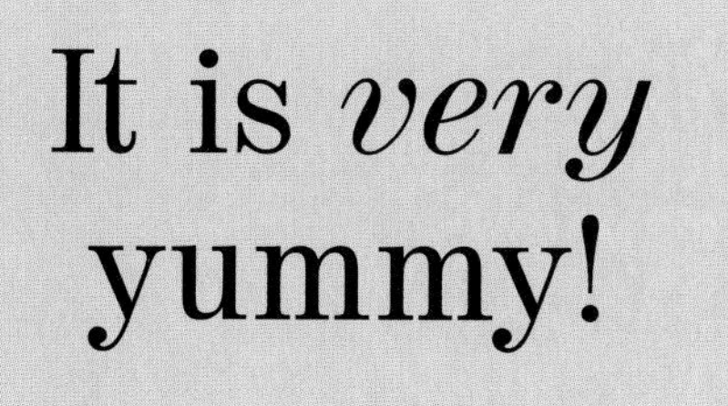
It is *very* yummy!

I will share
my ice cream.

It will not
be easy.

Hey…

Piggie is not here.

She does not know
I have ice cream.

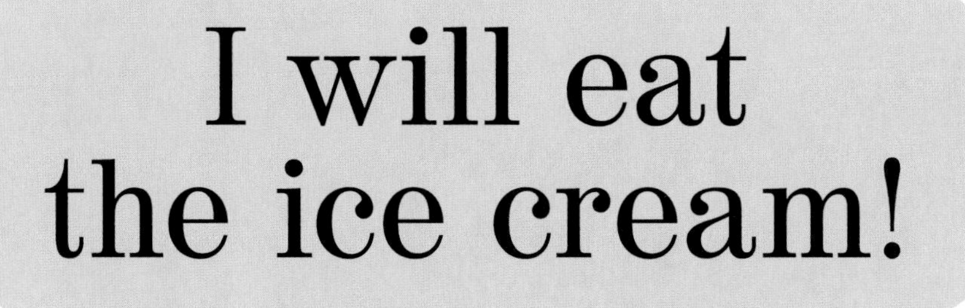
I will eat
the ice cream!

Where *is* Piggie?

What if she is
sad somewhere?

I must find her!

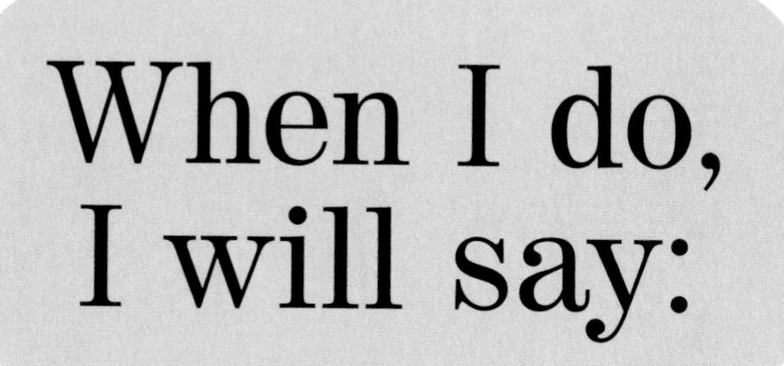
When I do,
I will say:

Would you like some of my ice cream?

Then she
will say:

Thank you!
That would cheer
me up!

Then I will give her my ice cream to share!

YUM!

Then my best friend
will be happy!

I will do it!
I will share my—

ice cream?

NOOOO

OOOOO!

Now Piggie cannot have
any of my ice cream!

Now *I* cannot
have any of
my ice cream!

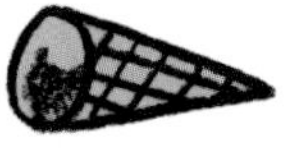

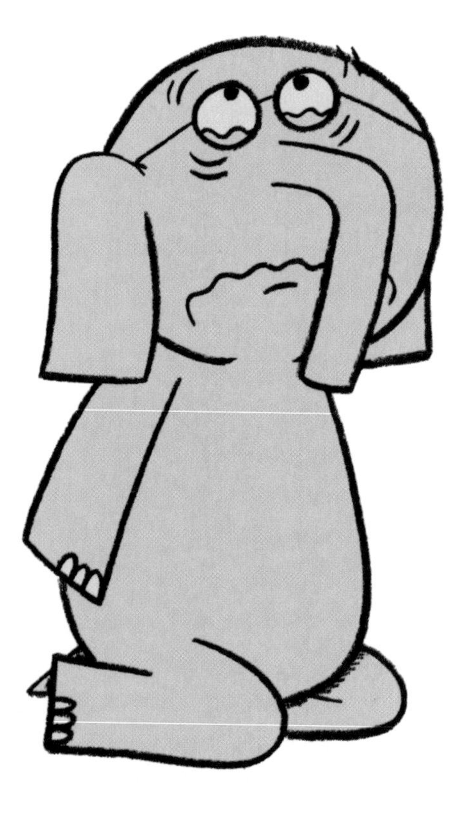

I blew it.

You look sad.
Would you like some
of my ice cream?

Thank you!
That would cheer
me up!

YUM!

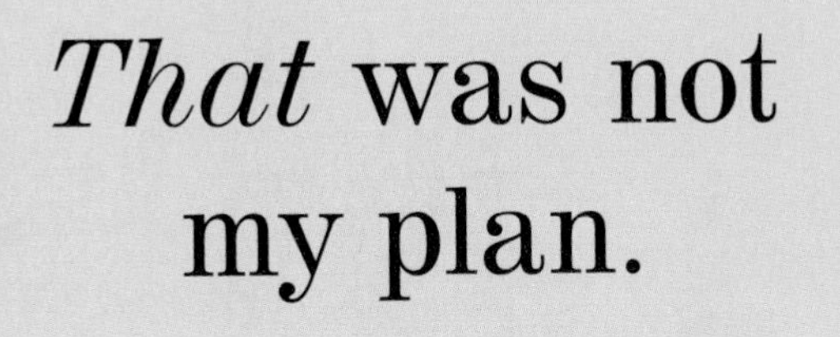
That was not
my plan.

Oh, well...

This
works too.

Have you read all of Elephant and Piggie's funny adventures?

Today I Will Fly!
My Friend Is Sad
I Am Invited to a Party!
There Is a Bird on Your Head!
(Theodor Seuss Geisel Medal)
I Love My New Toy!
I Will Surprise My Friend!
Are You Ready to Play Outside?
(Theodor Seuss Geisel Medal)
Watch Me Throw the Ball!
Elephants Cannot Dance!
Pigs Make Me Sneeze!
I Am Going!
Can I Play Too?
We Are in a Book!
(Theodor Seuss Geisel Honor)
I Broke My Trunk!
(Theodor Seuss Geisel Honor)
Should I Share My Ice Cream?
Happy Pig Day!
Listen to My Trumpet!
Let's Go for a Drive!
(Theodor Seuss Geisel Honor)
A Big Guy Took My Ball!
(Theodor Seuss Geisel Honor)
I'm a Frog!
My New Friend Is So Fun!
Waiting Is Not Easy!
(Theodor Seuss Geisel Honor)
I Will Take a Nap!
I *Really* Like Slop!
The Thank You Book